W9-CCT-630

goodbye, charlie

CHILDREN'S DEPT.
Rockville Public Library
Rockville, Ct. 06066

Charlie

goodbye, charlie

by evelyn bolton
illustrated by
john keely

CREATIVE EDUCATION, MANKATO, MINNESOTA

Published by Creative Education, 123 South Broad Street,
P. O. Box 227, Mankato, Minnesota 56001
Copyright© 1974 by Creative Education. International copyrights
reserved in all countries. No part of this book may be reproduced in any form
without written permission from the publisher.
Printed in the United States.
Distributed by Childrens Press, 1224 West Van Buren Street, Chicago, Illinois 60607

Library of Congress Number: 74-9572   ISBN: 0-87191-369-0

Library of Congress Cataloging in Publication Data
Bolton, Evelyn.   Goodbye, Charlie.
SUMMARY: When their horse is sold because she and her sister are getting
too big for him, Ellen finds it difficult to accept a new horse in his place.
(1. Horses—Fiction) I. Keely, John, illus. II. Title.
PZ7.B63598Go (Fic) 74-9572   ISBN 0-87191-369-0

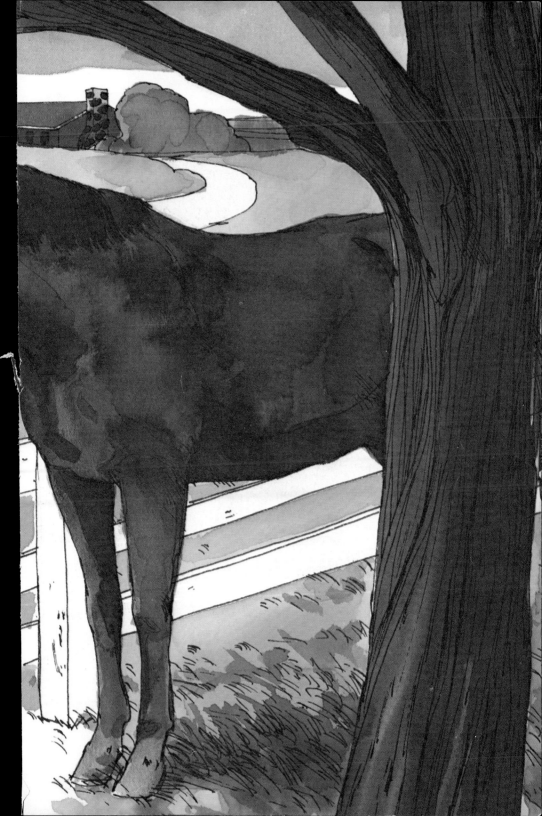

Ellen walked down the moonlit path behind the house. Tree shadows lay across the short grass of the corral, and there were the busy sounds of crickets in the summer shrubbery.

The corral fence still held the heat of the day's sun. Ellen leaned across it. She whistled once, a low, soft whistle that set one of the shadows to moving, hurrying toward her.

"Here, Charlie," she called. "Here." And the small horse was beside her, his black, black coat silver tipped by moonlight.

He took in two snapping bites the carrot she offered, his nose nudging her hand, begging for more.

"Old Greedy," Ellen said. She rubbed her cheek against his head, feeling the whisper of his warm breath on her throat, knowing the horse smell of him that was all grass and sweet hay and summer sunshine.

"Oh, Charlie, what am I going to do without you?"

Behind her the kitchen door opened and closed, and she stiffened, listening. She wanted no one to come, no one to tell her again how it had to be, and how there was no way, no way they could keep Charlie and the new horse, too. She recognized her dad's cough; but she didn't turn or speak, not even when he stopped at the railing beside her.

Charlie nickered a soft greeting, and Ellen saw her dad's hand move to rub Charlie's neck. Still she said nothing.

Her dad sighed. "I'm sorry, honey. I really am. Charlie's been a part of the family for a long time."

"Six years." Ellen heard the coldness in her voice, and it seemed impossible that

7

she could be speaking and feeling this way about her father.

"Six years and three months." Her dad's hands slid across the fence rail. "I remember when we decided to buy him. And I remember building the corral, and the shelter—all of us helping—your mother, Mia, even you, though you were so little."

Ellen watched a small bat, like a Halloween cut-out, circle and sweep against the moon. She remembered, too, the sawing and the hammering, and the piled up pieces of lumber in the back yard. She hadn't been tall enough to see over the fence when it was finished. Her first glimpse of Charlie had been through the rails; and he'd looked so big, so very big. But he wasn't, and that was the problem. Ellen and Mia had grown, but Charlie hadn't.

"Dad?" She gripped the rail tight. "Isn't there any way we can keep him?"

Her dad took a deep breath. "No, honey. Not with hay the price it is, and the shoeing, and the vet bills . . ." He stopped. "We really can't afford one horse, never mind two."

"Well then, let's just keep Charlie. We don't need . . ."

"It wouldn't be fair to Mia, or to you, or to Charlie." Her dad put his hand over hers. "Charlie needs to be ridden. You two big, leggy girls don't fit on him anymore. And you know what the judge told Mia at last month's show. Her riding was good, and Charlie performed well; but he's too small for her. You heard the judge tell Mia yourself."

"Mia! Who cares about Mia and her silly old horse shows? All she wants is to win a trophy and have blue ribbons and get her picture in the paper. She doesn't give a darn about Charlie." Ellen felt the tight ache under her ears as she tried to hold back the tears.

"That's not true." Her father stepped back, and his voice had lost its softness. "Mia loves Charlie as much as you do. She's more realistic, that's all. Maybe you should think about who's really being selfish."

Ellen heard his footsteps on the path back to the house. She couldn't stand it anymore! Being with Charlie for the last time was too awful to bear.

"Goodbye, Charlie," she whispered. She saw his face through a strange, bright blur; and then she was running back to the house with its lighted windows, up the winding stairs to her room.

Tomorrow night there would be a strange horse in Charlie's shelter—a seven-year-old, show-trained, a real beauty.

"Wait till you see him, Ellen," Mia had said. "He's a great looking chestnut, and he's so well trained. They let me ride him; and all you have to do is give him the littlest cue, and he knows just what to do."

"Sounds like a robot," Ellen had said. "You can have him."

She lay in bed now, wide-eyed, thinking about tomorrow. The man who had bought Charlie would come early for him, maybe before breakfast. Ellen wouldn't watch him go. She couldn't. Then later, her mom and dad and Mia would go to get THE OTHER HORSE.

Ellen turned her face to the wall. She'd pretend to be asleep when Mia came up—silly Mia, who'd started putting rollers in her hair and goop on her face and doing all those puffing and blowing exercises that were supposed to make her have some kind of terrific figure. Ellen squeezed her eyes tight closed. Mia had changed. Everything had changed.

She didn't need to pretend after all, because she didn't hear Mia come to bed. She was asleep; and when she woke, it was suddenly and magically morning.

Mia's bed was rumpled and empty. There was noise in the yard below the open bedroom window, and voices and the sound of a car door slamming.

Ellen tiptoed to look from behind the curtains.

Her mom and dad were talking with a man who stood by a horse trailer hitched to a blue car. The man had a bald head with freckles across the top of it. Freckles!

"It would be better if you turned around and backed the trailer up to the corral gate," Ellen's dad said. "He'll load easier that way."

Ellen swallowed. She licked the new mosquito bite on her wrist. They were ready to load Charlie.

The man climbed into the car and backed up very neatly, and then Ellen saw Mia leading Charlie across the corral. Mia still had her fat pink rollers in her hair. Ellen was careful not to look at Charlie. She hid her face against the white blur of the curtains.

"Don't you think we should call Ellen?" That was her mother, soft and anxious.

"No. It's better this way." Her father sounded firm and matter-of-fact.

Charlie's hooves clattered on the path.

"Come on, fellow. Up you go." That was Mia's voice.

Trailer doors closed. She heard the clang of the bolt going across.

Ellen peeped from behind the curtain. The man and her dad were shaking hands.

"Any time you folks want to visit him, you're more than welcome. It's the house right at the end of Green View Street, the one with the big oak tree in the front yard."

"Take good care of him," Ellen's

mom said, and Ellen saw her dad put his arm around her mom's waist. Mia was snuffling.

Mr. Freckle Head edged the car out of the driveway, and Ellen could see he knew how to handle a trailer.

She got dressed and went slowly downstairs.

"Remember how she was when Ginger died?" Her mother's voice came through the kitchen door. "She moped and moped."

"And then we got another dog; and it took a while, but she got over it." Her dad sounded confident. "Ellen will be all right."

They were talking about her. They thought she'd get over Charlie, but they were wrong.

She sat at the kitchen table, slurping her cornflakes on purpose, knowing it was gross and that no one was going to get mad at her today. She could probably eat the cornflakes with her hands if she wanted to, and nobody would say anything. And nobody did, except Mia who whispered,

"Brat!" as Ellen walked past her on the way out. Ellen slammed the door. Brat yourself!

She unlocked her bicycle and rode to Lacy Park, sitting on the dappled grass under a tree, thinking about Charlie. Remembering. She waited till the sun moved all the way through the leaves of the tree before she left. Her stomach growled, and she knew it was past lunch time.

There was no wind to move the heat

around, and she rode slowly. She left her bike at the back door. Was the new horse here already?

There was no one in the kitchen. Ellen poured herself a glass of milk and took a handful of peanut butter cookies. Maybe they were down in the corral. There would be no harm in slipping down to have a look. If she kept behind Charlie's shelter, they wouldn't see her.

She circled the garage, crouched low and ran for the shelter, pressing herself against its smooth, hot wood.

"Ellen? Is that you, honey?"

How could her mother possibly have seen or heard her? Did all mothers have those extra eyes that went all the way around their heads? Mothers and teachers! Ellen came out.

"Come and meet Finn," her father said.

"I don't want to." She couldn't understand why her feet were taking her across the corral when she'd just said she didn't want to go.

"Isn't he super?" Mia asked.

"He's all right." Ellen kept her hands in the pockets of her jeans so they would behave. There was something about a horse that begged to be touched. She clenched her fists.

He was the deep copper color of her dad's riding boots when he'd just polished them. He was beautiful, beautiful; and he was bridled with Charlie's bridle, and that was Charlie's saddle on his back.

"He's got mean eyes," Ellen said.

"Oh, pooh!" Mia swung herself up and into the saddle. "Come on, Finn. Let's see how we do."

Ellen watched them from under the shade of her hand. Mia walked the horse, and then asked him to trot. He obeyed immediately.

"He's good," Ellen's mom said.

"And he's just the right size." Her dad's voice held satisfaction. "There's room for the girls to grow. We won't have *that* problem again."

Ellen swallowed. *That* problem! He meant Charlie. That's all Charlie had been at the end. *That* problem!

Mia trotted toward them and reined in. The heat had made her face shiny. "He's great. We'll hardly need to teach him a thing. You want to try him, Ellen?"

"No, thanks." Ellen yawned to show how bored she was. "I don't like robot horses."

She heard Mia's voice as she walked away. "Don't pay any attention, Mom. She's sulking, that's all."

"And you know what you are, all of you," Ellen thought. "You're disloyal, and you're hateful. Go ahead and forget Charlie. Your old horse has mean eyes. Real mean." She turned on the T.V. in the den and curled up in a corner of the couch. If they wanted to think she was sulking, it was OK with her. She'd sulk for the rest of the summer if she wanted to.

It was hard to stay sulky though. After a few days no one seemed to notice. All the kids on the street came to visit the other horse, and they and Mia stayed most of the time in the corral, working with him. Ellen kept away.

"Are you going to spend your whole vacation in front of that television?" her mom asked.

Ellen shrugged. "Nothing else to do."

It was that night that her dad issued the new orders. "I'm getting tired of this, Ellen. We've put up with your nonsense long enough. It's not fair that Mia has to do everything for Finn. Starting tomorrow you'll take over his feeding, and you've got to help clean out the shelter and groom him, too, the way you did for Charlie."

"But he's not Charlie, and he's not my horse, and . . ."

"Starting tomorrow." When her dad looked at her like that, there was no point in arguing. She'd do it. But she didn't have to like it.

Finn had a way of nickering and nuzzling at her when she brought down his morning oats, and she would push his head aside and dump his oats and change his water and keep her hands off him, and her eyes off him, too, as much as possible.

She helped Mia with his grooming, cleaning out his feet with the hoof pick, checking his eyes and his nose as coldly as a stranger, seeing that his tack was rubbed and polished. But she never offered, ever, to brush him or curry him, afraid of the sweet silly feeling that was growing stronger inside of her day by day, however much she tried to push it away. It was easy enough to push away Finn's head, but how did you push away longings inside of you that you couldn't see and couldn't reach?

"Robot horse," she told herself.

"Taking Charlie's place." And she said the words over and over each time she got near him.

One evening, after dinner, Mia called to ask whether she could spend the night with a friend, and their mom said yes.

Ellen's dad looked up at her over the top of his paper. "You'll have to go down and blanket Finn. It's going to be cooler tonight. Better do it now in case you forget."

"Why me? That's Mia's job. You should make her come home and do it. He's her horse."

"Do it." All she could see was the paper, but even the paper looked angry.

Ellen walked slowly down the path to the corral. Tree shadows lay across the short grass, and the crickets were still busy in the shrubbery. It was night; and it was the way it had always been, so many nights, so many times . . . except that Charlie didn't come from the shadows, trotting toward her.

She opened the corral gate and saw that Finn stood patiently in the shelter.

"Old smarty," Ellen said coldly. "I suppose you knew you were going to be blanketed. Robot horse!"

She took the blanket from its shelf and spread it across his back, bringing the straps down under his stomach. He was warm and soft, his stomach swelling gently under her hands. She felt him nuzzle her hair, tugging a little.

"Go away," Ellen said. Then she stumbled up, smelling the sleepy horse smell of him; and her hands were suddenly on his head, her cheek against his neck, and she was crying, so hard she couldn't seem to stop.

"Oh, Charlie," she said; and she tried to remember the little black horse, to catch the memory of him and hold it, for it was fading, blurring, changing, to become not Charlie, but Finn.

Hiccups caught at her throat as she ran back to the house and up to her room. She threw herself across the bed.

Three weeks! Just three weeks, and Charlie was forgotten. "I won't forget him; I won't," she thought. "I'll go see him." She sat up and blew her nose, suddenly happier. Green View Street. She could do it easily on her bicycle. Why hadn't she gone to see him before? Because it would hurt too much, that was why. So how could she go now? She didn't know.

In the early morning she unblanketed Finn, fed him his oats and changed his water, holding herself tight inside, not letting herself think.

"I'll be gone for a while," she told her mom; and she got her bicycle and rode through the quiet, tree-lined streets. Newspapers lay unopened in front yards. Birds called to her from telephone wires.

Green View Street was still asleep. The oak tree had two canvas swings hanging from its lower branches, and there was a bicycle with training wheels lying by the front porch.

Ellen walked round the side of the house and saw a corral at the bottom of a steep slope.

A woman in a blue bathrobe opened a window. "Good morning."

"Hi! I'm Ellen Walden. We used to own Charlie. Is it all right if I go see him?"

"Help yourself." Mrs. Freckle Head smiled. "The kids are there already."

Ellen walked down the slope. Why was her heart beating so fast? Why was she suddenly afraid? Then she saw Charlie. Dear, sweet Charlie! She stopped. But he was so small! She hadn't remembered he was *that* small.

A boy and a girl were feeding him apples from a red plastic bucket.

"Charlie," Ellen called, and the children's heads turned. Charlie's ears twitched.

Ellen gave her low, soft whistle; and he came at a trot, the children running behind him, apples bumping and tumbling from the red bucket.

Ellen rubbed his head. "Too many apples aren't good for him," she told the little boy. "One's all right." She smiled. "Charlie used to belong to me," she explained.

"Oh." The boy looked anxious. "But he's ours now." He put a possessive hand on Charlie's rump.

"I know." Ellen looked at them. The boy and his sister were the size she and Mia had been when they first got Charlie. She looked again, and it was as though she saw the three of them through a camera lens, perfectly in balance — the little boy, the little girl and the little black horse.

"Why did you sell him?" the boy asked. "Didn't you like him anymore?"

"Of course we liked him. It's just . . . things change. We grew too big. We had to let him go."

She saw the understanding on the little boy's face. He believed her. Of course he believed her. It was the truth. *We had to let him go.* She was dazed at how simple it was. She would always love Charlie. But there was no need to feel guilty or ashamed because she was beginning to love Finn, too.

"We like Charlie a lot," the little girl said.

"I know," Ellen smiled. "How can you help loving a horse when he's your horse," she thought. "How can you help it?"

"Goodbye, Charlie," she said. "I'll come back and see you. I'll come back often." And somehow it wasn't like the last time she'd told him goodbye. A part of the hurt was still there, but it was easier now; and she knew why she was hurrying, hurrying up the slope, hurrying, hurrying home.

creative
education

horse
stories
by
evelyn
bolton

Removed

ROCKVILLE PUBLIC LIBRARY

3 4035 04405 9620

♣J ✓
BOL

Bolton, Evelyn
Goodbye, Charlie

CHILDREN'S DEPT.
Rockville Public Library
Rockville, Ct. 06066